Dragons
Activity Book

Jessica Mazurkiewicz

DOVER PUBLICATIONS, INC.
Mineola, New York

Bibliographical Note

Dragons Activity Book is a new work, first published by Dover Publications, Inc., in 2011.

International Standard Book Number

ISBN-13: 978-0-486-47521-9
ISBN-10: 0-486-47521-2

Manufactured in the United States by LSC Communications
47521205   2017
www.doverpublications.com

Note

Dragons are huge reptile-like creatures that possess magical qualities. They played an important role in some cultures and have been a subject of fantasy for many centuries. In this book are 41 activities featuring some playful dragons, medieval serpents, and baby dragons. You will find secret codes, spot-the differences, mazes, and many other puzzles that will bring you into the mythical world of dragons. If you need help with a puzzle, or if you want to check your answers, the solutions begin on page 54. And after you're through solving all the puzzles, you can color them any way you choose!

Circle the two dragons above that are exactly the same.

Count how many teeth are in the dragon's mouth
and fill the number into the blank space on the cloud.

W=1 N=2 G=3 S=4 L=5 A=6 O=7

Dragons usually have

1	9	2	3	4

and strong

13	5	6	1	4

The wizard wants to tell you some things about dragons.

U=8 I=9 R=10 E=11 F=12 C=13 P=14

Be careful if you meet a dragon!

They are known to be

14	7	1	11	10	12	8	5

,

12	11	10	7	13	9	7	8	4

and tricky!

Use the letter and number code to fill in the blanks.

Connect the dots from 1 through 20 to make the
dragon breathe fire.

DRAGON

drag

Using only the letters in the word Dragon,
spell out as many words as you can.
One word has been filled in to start you off.

The Mother dragon has hidden her seven eggs near the volcano. Can you find and circle all of them?

Unscramble the letters on the flames and fill them
into the blanks to learn what a dragon's skin is covered in.

Help the dragon count his treasure by counting how many there are of each item and fill the number into the blank space provided next to it.

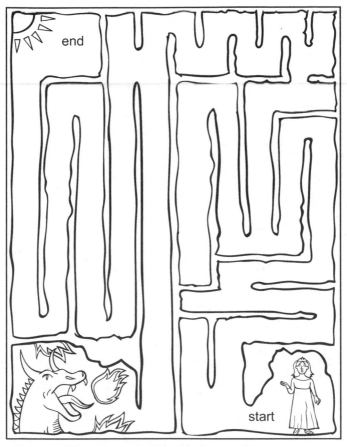

end

start

Guide the princess from the start to the end of the
cave maze so that she can escape the dragon's lair.

Look carefully at the two pictures of a dragon
and a knight.

Circle the six things that make this picture different
from the picture on the left.

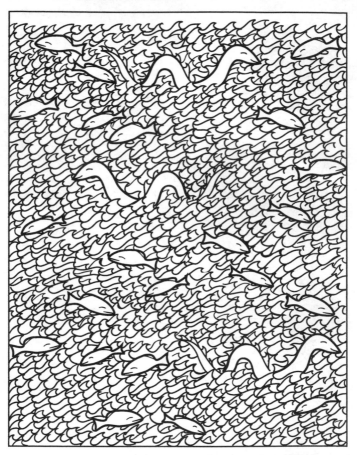

Can you find and circle the three water dragons
that are hiding in the waves?

Some baby dragons just hatched! Count the
number of eggs that haven't hatched yet and fill the
number into the space on the dragon's belly.

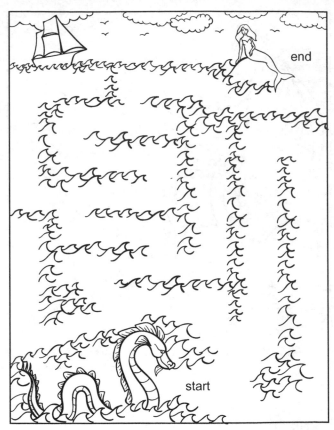

end

start

Can you help the dragon reach his friend the mermaid by guiding him from the start to the end of the wave maze?

Follow the trails and circle the samurai that has a path
to reach the dragon.

O=1 F=2 Y=3 S=4 A=5

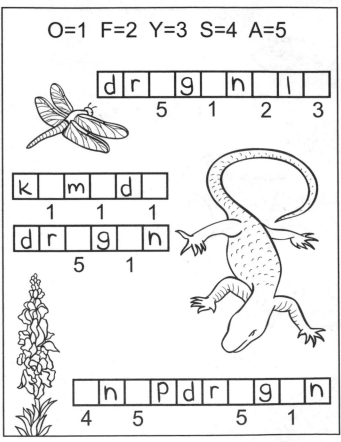

d	r		g		n		l
	5		1		2		3

k		m		d	
1		1		1	

d	r		g		n
	5		1		

	n		p	d	r		g		n
4		5				5		1	

Use the number code to fill in the blanks and learn the
names of an insect, animal and flower that are
named after dragons.

20

Color the picture using the letter code.
B=Blue   G=Green   O=Orange   R=Red   Y=Yellow

Find and circle the letters D, R, A, G, O and N that
are hidden in the picture above.

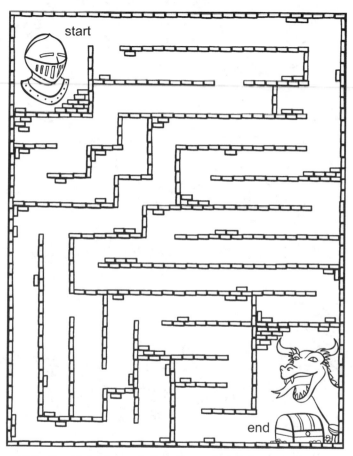

Help the Knight reach the dragon's lair by guiding him from the start to the end of the dungeon maze.

23

Count how many bursts of fire surround the dragon
and fill the number into the space provided in the cloud.

```
D R A G O N D R A D O
R W Y R V G T I U R E
A I X B J O X N N A I
G N B U E L D G S G L
I G A T E D R A G O N
O D R A F R A F L N D
D T R E S A G U Z E R
R N R A O G O P D O A
A W E F O O N L R S G
G D A L N N L D A A E
O O G Y A A C T G R R
N A E Z R I S P O H F
F G L D R A G O N B L
L N A G O N E R F L Y
Y C V R A D R A G O N
```

The word DRAGON is hidden in the crossword 9 times.
Search vertically and horizontally to find them all.

Look carefully at the two pictures of
a dragon resting in castle ruins.

Circle the six things that make this picture different
from the picture on the left.

Connect the dots from 1 through 26 to see
Draco, the dragon that lives among the stars.

The dragon has a warning for you. Arrange the
words from her eggs into the blanks below to read it.

end

start

Help the dragon get from the start
to the end of the lightning maze.

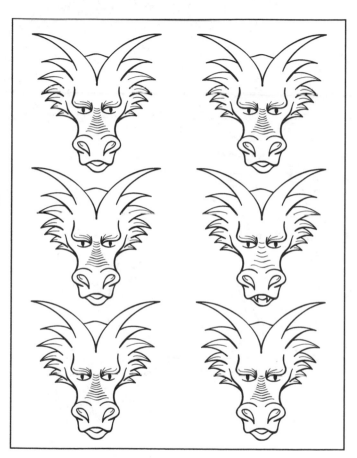

Look carefully at the dragons above and circle
the one that is different from the rest.

Count how many spots are on the dragon and fill
the number into the blank space on the mirror.

pegasus

gryphon [2]

harpy

dragon

phoenix

Place the mythical beasts above in alphabetical order by filling a number in each blank square. One square has been filled in to get you started.

Circle which of the baby dragons will fit into the empty space in the flame at the bottom of the page.

Connect the dots from 1 through 13 to
complete the dragon shown above.

Connect the dots from 1 through 18 to
give the dragon a perch.

Guide the fire breathing dragon from the
start to the end of the cloud maze.

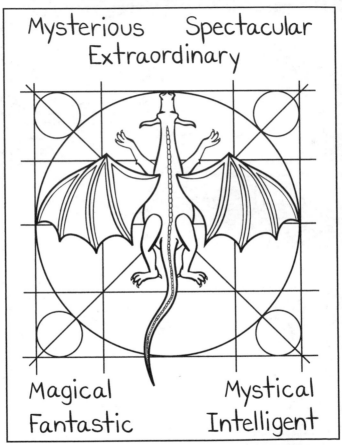

Mysterious   Spectacular
Extraordinary

Magical   Mystical
Fantastic   Intelligent

Some words that describe a dragon are listed
above. Search for them in the crossword on the right.

```
R I N T E M L L Y N P
S M F R V Y T E U H E
P I A B J S X I N O X
E B N G E T I N S B T
C G T R I I L T C K R
T V A D E C R E L Y A
A T S E S A A L Z E O
C N T R M L R L H O R
U W I F O L L I E S D
L P C L N Y L G L A I
A X G Y A A C E A R N
R A E Z R I S N U H A
F L L E C L W T I B R
M Y S T E R I O U S Y
Y C T T V R A E G M N
```

Search the crossword vertically, horizontally and
diagonally to find and circle the listed words.

39

Look carefully at the two pictures of the dragon with her nest and the castle in the clouds.

Circle the six things that make this picture different
from the picture on the left.

The number next to each dragon tells how many teeth should be in his mouth. Can you complete each of the dragons by drawing teeth? One dragon has been completed to get you started.

Look carefully at the items surrounding the dragon.
Circle the objects he will add to his treasure collection.

DRAGON

gol☐

fi☐e

m☐at

sc☐le

k☐ight

Use each letter from the word DRAGON one time
to complete each of the words shown next to a picture.
One blank has been filled in to get you started.

Dragons come in many different colors.
Color the dragons above in using the number code.
1=Blue   2=Green   3=Red   4=Yellow

45

R=1 K=2 C=3 P=4 E=5 N=6 S=7 A=8

Wyverns are snake-like

3 1 5 8 10 12 15 5 7

with

13 9 6 11 7

and two legs.

The dragon wants to tell you some things
about his cousin, the Wyvern.

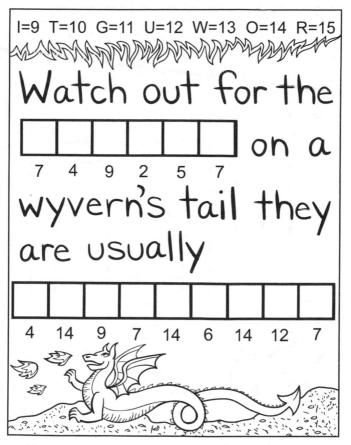

Watch out for the

7	4	9	2	5	7

on a

wyvern's tail they
are usually

4	14	9	7	14	6	14	12	7

Use the letter and number code to fill in the blanks.

Only one of the knights has a path through the maze.
Try to guide each knight through the maze and circle
the one that has a path to the dragon's lair.

Count the spikes on each of the dragons shown above
and circle the dragon with the most spikes.

Look carefully at the two pictures of dragons
resting near a rainbow.

Circle the six things that make this picture different
from the picture on the left.

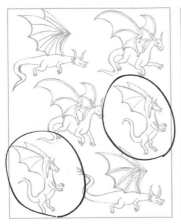

page 4

24

page 5

W=1 N=2 G=3 S=4 L=5 A=6 O=7

Dragons usually have

| w | i | n | g | s |
| 1 | 9 | 2 | 3 | 4 |

and strong

| c | l | a | w | s |
| 13 | 5 | 6 | 1 | 4 |

.

page 6

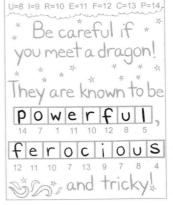

U=8 I=9 R=10 E=11 F=12 C=13 P=14

Be careful if you meet a dragon!

They are known to be

| p | o | w | e | r | f | u | l |
| 14 | 7 | 1 | 11 | 10 | 12 | 8 | 5 |

,

| f | e | r | o | c | i | o | u | s |
| 12 | 11 | 10 | 7 | 13 | 9 | 7 | 8 | 4 |

and tricky!

page 7

page 8

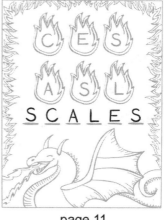

page 9

page 10

page 11

page 12

page 13

page 15

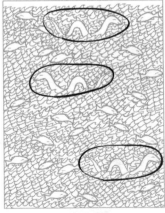

page 16

page 17

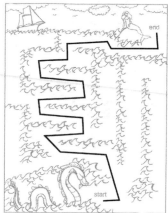

page 18

page 19

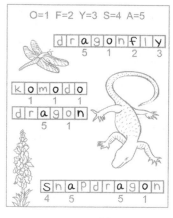

page 20

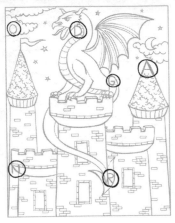

page 22

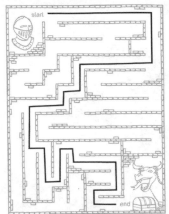

page 23

page 24

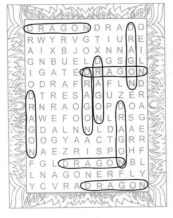

page 25

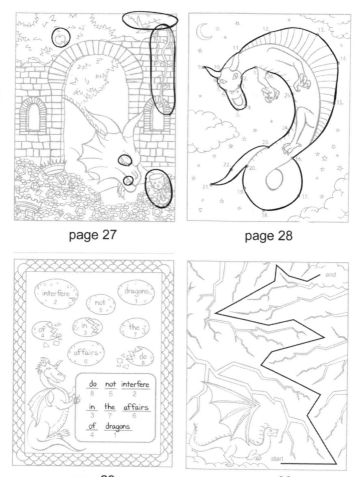

page 27

page 28

page 29

page 30

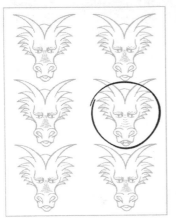

page 31

page 32

page 33

page 34

page 35

page 36

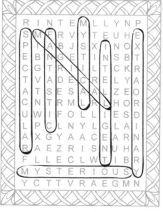

page 37

page 39

page 41

page 43

page 44

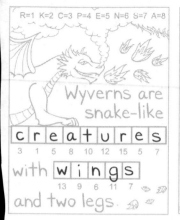

R=1 K=2 C=3 P=4 E=5 N=6 S=7 A=8

Wyverns are snake-like

c	r	e	a	t	u	r	e	s
3	1	5	8	10	12	15	5	7

with

w	i	n	g	s
13	9	6	11	7

and two legs.

page 46

I=9 T=10 G=11 U=12 W=13 O=14 R=15

Watch out for the

s	p	i	k	e	s
7	4	9	2	5	7

on a wyvern's tail they are usually

p	o	i	s	o	n	o	u	s
4	14	9	7	14	6	14	12	7

page 47

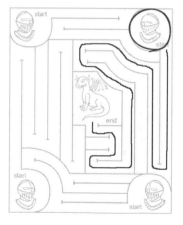

start

start

end

start

start

page 48

page 49

page 51